SWAN LIBRARY
4 North Main Street
Albion, NY 14411-1241

MW00955575

Cuento de Luz (Tale of Light) publishes stories that enlighten our lives to bring out our inner child. Stories that make time stand still for us to live the present. Stories that take the imagination on a journey and help care for our planet, to respect differences, break down barriers and promote peace. Stories that do not leave you indifferent; stories that lift you up.

Cuento de Luz respects the environment and contributes to the protection of nature, incorporating sustainability principles through eco-friendly publishing.

CUENTO
DE LUZ

Yago's Heartbeat

All rights reserved. Unless provided by law, no part of this book may be reproduced, distributed, publicly communicated or transformed in any way without the authorisation of the publisher.

© 2010 CUENTO DE LUZ SL
Calle Claveles 10
Urb. Monteclaro
Pozuelo de Alarcon
28223 Madrid, Spain

www.cuentodeluz.com

Text © Conchita Miranda
Illustrations © Monica Carretero
English translation by Jon Brokenbrow

ISBN: 978-84-938240-3-7
DL: M-47454-2010

Printed by Graficas AGA in Madrid, Spain,
November 2010, print number 65691

6\11

LIGHT Series

To my father, who passed on his love of books to me.
To Ramón, my great companion in this adventure.
Thanks to Belén and a team of wonderful women for their
enthusiasm and dedication in publishing this story.

sobre ruedas
Fundación de Ayuda al Paralítico Cerebral

The author donates all proceeds from this book to
the "Sobre Ruedas" Foundation for children with cerebral palsy.
www.fundacionsobreruedas.org

Yago's Heartbeat

Conchita Miranda

CUENTO
DE LUZ

Illustrations by Monica Carretero

It all began a long, long time ago, in the deep blue sea where I was
born, surrounded by coral and fish of every imaginable color.
I was born small and that's the way I stayed, small: just a little snail.
Compared to my sisters, I was just a little speck. That's why,
whenever we were washed up onto the beach,
I was always thrown back into the sea.

But one day, everything changed. It was a peaceful winter day, one of those days when the sun tries to break through the chill with its warming rays. I was covered in sand, waiting to be found and then thrown back into the sea as usual, when suddenly a rough, weathered hand picked me up, brushed of the sand, and I saw a face smiling down at me. You see, I wasn't just small. I also had a strange, twisted hole in my shell, and that made me different.

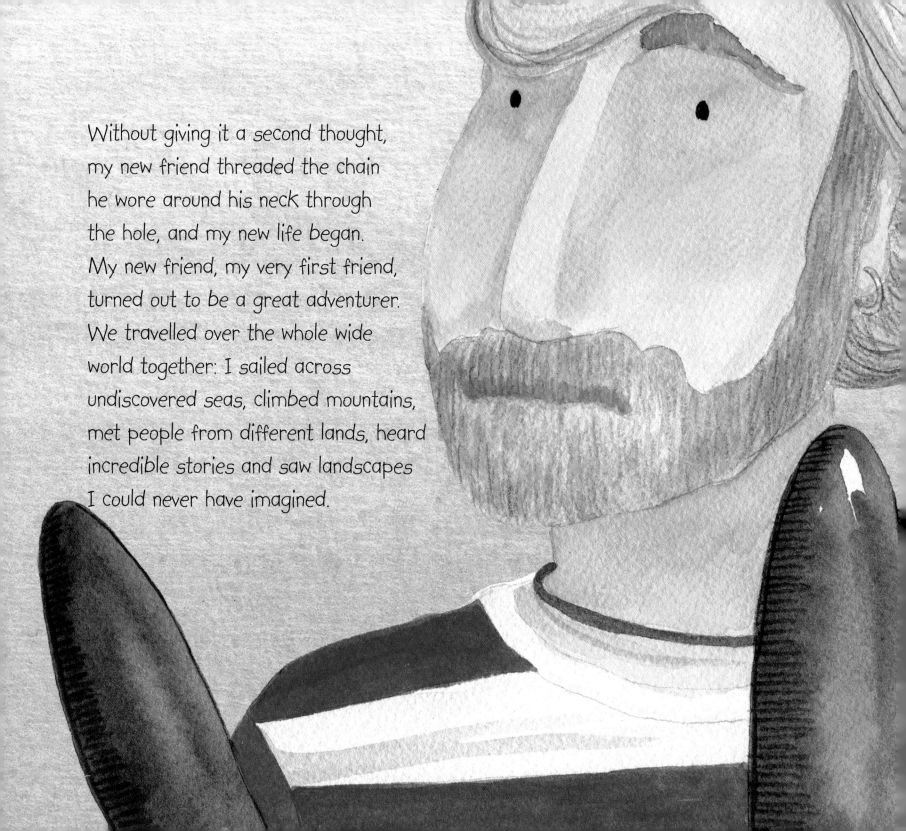

Without giving it a second thought,
my new friend threaded the chain
he wore around his neck through
the hole, and my new life began.
My new friend, my very first friend,
turned out to be a great adventurer.
We travelled over the whole wide
world together: I sailed across
undiscovered seas, climbed mountains,
met people from different lands, heard
incredible stories and saw landscapes
I could never have imagined.

I had become used to this busy life, full of adventures and surprises, but what I didn't know is that there were others waiting for me that were very different from those I'd shared with my friend.

The years went by, not just for my old friend, but also for his chain, which hung around his thick, strong neck.

Like him, the years were gradually wearing it away.
One day, almost without realizing it, while we were walking along the beach
I slid off, without making any noise, without being able to warn him.
The chain broke, and I returned to the sand.

I no longer felt his touch, his warmth.
Farewell to my adventures, to my friend....
I saw how he gradually faded into the distance
with his weary walk, unaware that his old travelling
companion, his little snail, had been left behind
on that vast, empty beach.

My old friend had barely disappeared from view, when suddenly the small, soft hand of a child, with its nimble and slightly grubby fingers, plucked me away from that gloomy scene. He blew and blew on my shell. "What a pretty one!" he thought, and put me in his pocket.

When he arrived home and picked me up again, he saw my little hole and said to me, "Wow! You're different, like Yago. You have to meet him."

And that's how I ended up hanging around the neck of a little boy called Yago.

I gradually realized that this time things were going to be different.
This new boy, my new, young friend, couldn't walk.
He was in a wheelchair, and he couldn't talk, either!

I couldn't believe it. After living through a thousand adventures with my old friend,
now I was going to be sat in a chair, faced with a life of silence and boredom.

While I was lost in my thoughts, and more than a little confused about
this new situation...

"Well, look at this! Where did this lovely shell come from?"

It was a sweet, gentle voice, and when I saw her smile I realized that she could
only be Yago's mother. After feeling so sorry for myself, it was nice to feel her
presence, and especially to hear her flattering remark.

But things were about to change...

"I found her on the beach. Isn't she pretty?
Look, she's got a little hole. She's special, just like Yago.
That's why I gave her to him, as he likes the sea so much."

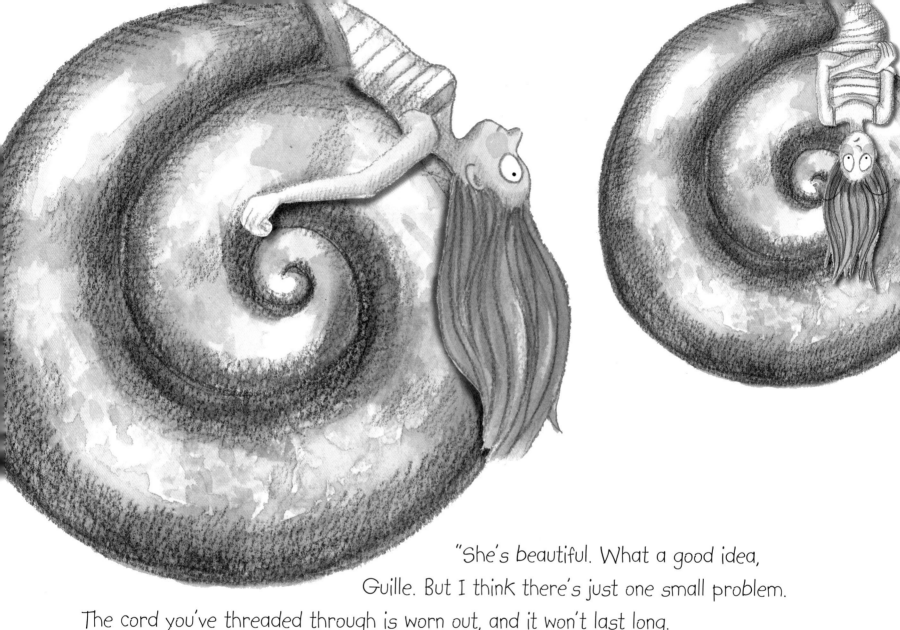

"She's beautiful. What a good idea,
Guille. But I think there's just one small problem.
The cord you've threaded through is worn out, and it won't last long.
It would be a pity if she fell off, but don't worry.
Before he goes to the beach tomorrow I'll find a nice, strong one,
so he'll never lose her."

Never! Suddenly, that sweet, smiling mother had become my jailer.

Never. I would always be hung around the neck of the silent child.

I tried to calm down and think. There was still hope.

The cord was very old, and with luck it would snap: I had 24 hours left.

Silence returned, and I sank back into my memories.

The last great adventure had been on board a magnificent sailing ship, when we were

caught in a terrible storm... suddenly, the silence was broken: now it was his older sister.

Smothering Yago in kisses, she told him about the fun she'd had on the beach,

about the boys she'd seen.

Miriam, a typical teenager, forgot about herself for a moment to be with the silent child.

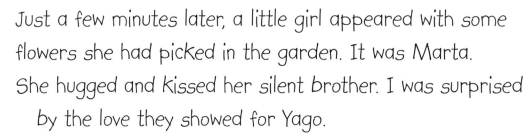

Just a few minutes later, a little girl appeared with some
flowers she had picked in the garden. It was Marta.
She hugged and kissed her silent brother. I was surprised
by the love they showed for Yago.
I have spent a lot of time near to humans,
I know how much they love to talk, to hug and kiss
to show how much they love each other, but I could
see that this wasn't the case with Yago at all.
Nevertheless, they all hugged him and kissed him,
and more besides.
They talked to him about everything,
about the things that made them sad,
the things that made them happy,
and even their secrets.

And so, I gradually began to see what had
started out so badly in a different light.

It was fun to meet each member of the family, each one different from the other,
with different stories, different laughter, but with something they all shared:
their great love and tenderness towards Yago.

But it didn't stop there. It wasn't just the family that loved him;
there were also his brother and sisters' friends, their parents...
every time someone came to the house, they'd always give Yago a kiss or a hug.
But what was it about Yago?

What I really had to do was to concentrate on Yago and find out what he did to be
so loved, although it wasn't easy with everything that was going on around me: from
Miriam's latest boyfriend, the goals that Guille had scored, or the flowers that
Marta was always finding. Other times it was his father tousling his hair,
or his mother whispering to him sweetly. Even the arguments were fun.

In fact, I was too absorbed to remember about Yago, the one I'd never heard
speak... until I decided to listen.

SWAN LIBRARY
4 North Main Street
Albion, NY 14411-1241

Darkness fell and everything was peaceful. The house was silent again.
Suddenly I saw a slight movement. The cord! I knew there was still hope,
that it was old and worn. With luck, it would break before he went to the beach
and I would be free again, free to return to my life of adventure.

But... I was still puzzled by this mysterious love for my silent friend.

As I was hanging around Yago's neck, I was close to his heart, and I could hear it
beating. Until that moment I hadn't noticed, distracted by all that noise.

And that night it happened. I heard his heartbeat. It was a special sound,
full of peace and calm. Lulled by that gentle symphony, I was just falling asleep,
when suddenly the rhythm changed.

It was a different heartbeat, secure and full of emotion, and at the same time with a shared, secret sweetness all of its own. And then Yago's father appeared. Secure, that was how the little boy felt with him. Nothing could harm him at his father's side.

Was that possible? A special language? The heartbeats...

Maybe it was just by chance. The idea of his heartbeats being a new language was just too strange. The best thing would be to sleep and wait until the following morning.

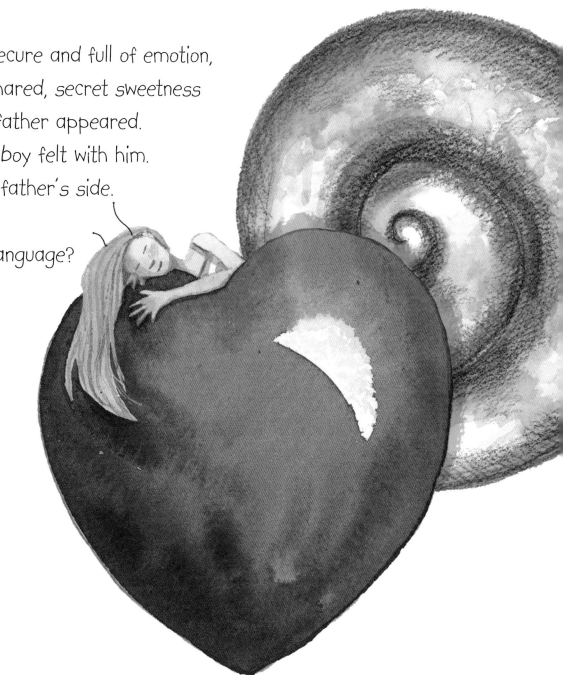

I was just falling asleep when the heartbeat, which had returned to its calm, peaceful pace, suddenly gave a start. It changed rhythm again.
This time it was joyful, innocent, and seemed to be moving in leaps and bounds.
Of course, it was Marta, who had had a nightmare and snuggled into bed alongside Yago for comfort. And little by little, we all fell asleep.

Was it possible? Yes, it was possible, it was real! My beloved Yago had a special language for each one of them. It was the most wonderful language I had ever heard in my long, busy life.
A silent language that came straight from the heart.

That morning, everything seemed different to me, and my head was full of questions. What were the heartbeats like for his mother, for Miriam, and for Guille?
Or had it just been a dream?
Would my cord break before
I found out all the answers?

In the midst of this sea of doubts, I suddenly heard the heartbeat change again:
this time the rhythm stayed the same, but instead it became more intense.
It was his mother! Completely in harmony with each other,
together from the very beginning, in unison, a single melody with different tones.

My jailer... and yet this melody was purer, more beautiful and more intense
than any I had heard in the wonderful theatres
I had visited with my old friend.

Yago, my beloved Yago, had a different
heartbeat for each one, and in that silence
I learned how to recognise them.

Another unmistakable sound was that funny, chaotic heartbeat.
It was Guille, and the heartbeat became calm and throbbed to the sound of the words he read from his storybook, as he sat next to Yago's bed.
That same chaotic rhythm continued as he told him about his favorite football team, or about the latest 'A' he'd got at school.

Suddenly, a deep, unique heartbeat announced
the arrival of Miriam. Like her, it was intense,
full of strength and vitality. Like any teenager,
always bursting with energy, she could go from
joy to tears in the blinking of an eye,
and Yago was always there to comfort her.

She'd tell him about everything: her latest boyfriend, her friends' secrets and her own, and in their eyes you could see that they understood each other.

And now I was beginning to understand. Yago did speak, but with his own, silent language, a language that came from deep within him.
I also understood that everyone heard and understood that language, even though they didn't know it.

With that new discovery, I woke up. All of those great adventures were behind me. Great? Now I laugh about that intense life. This really was intense.

Like I said, my great discovery was the start of everything.
There was a whole little world around Yago, although I found it hard to believe that I was seeing it and experiencing it.

That day was a school day. It was the end of June, and the children only had classes until midday. Later, in the afternoon, we would go down to the beach and I would be free.
Free? It was all so exciting... if only I had a little more time.

And I thought I knew it all. Entering the school, a wave of new surprises swept over me, more dizzying than any of the mountains I had climbed.

Everything started when we get out of the car.
A smile quickly appeared, with a teacher
behind it. It's never the same person,
but it's always the same smile:
gentle, caring and sincere.

A kiss from mum and we
were off through the door,
entering the best of worlds,
although to be quite honest
with you, it didn't seem like
that to me at the start.

I found that first smile to be warm and friendly from the very first moment, but what came next...

Boys and girls who were different from each other, and different from everyone else. I have to confess it was hard for me. Despite the fact that in the last few hours I'd discovered Yago's secret language and his inner world, I wasn't prepared for that new experience. Everything was so different to what I'd known until then. Some were in wheelchairs, others were walking with difficulty, some were talking, others were making sounds that were difficult to understand: it was a different world.

But there was something they all shared, something that brought them together, which had begun when we got out of the car: the smile. In the midst of all that noise, the to-and-fro of wheelchairs, the superhuman effort to get the best out of each and every one, there was always, always a common factor: a special joy that changed everything.

I opened my eyes and perked up my ears. I didn't want to miss a thing.

That day was the summer festival. Now these were actors.
I remembered all of the famous people I'd met throughout
my life, and I can tell you they had a lot to learn from
these children, who gave it their all within their
possibilities, bringing out the best in every one.

Can you dance in a wheelchair?
Can you sing without being able to speak?
Can you tell stories just with your eyes?
You can, believe me when I say you can.
I saw it, I heard it, I felt it...
And the spectators? With their enthusiasm,
those proud, emotional parents turned that
festival into the greatest show on earth.

Without doubt, it was the most
wonderful experience of my life.

I have struggled to the top of the highest peaks, I have seen incredible sunsets,
I have braved terrible storms in the middle of the ocean,
I have heard tales of tremendous bravery and courage, but...
I never imagined that from a wheelchair that you cannot even move on your own,
it would be possible to see and feel what I was experiencing.

We returned home, and before we went to the beach, we had a little nap.

There in the bed, surrounded by silence, feeling Yago's sweet, gentle heartbeat, I tried to put into perspective everything I'd seen over the last 24 hours.

Maybe he'd never climb a mountain, but learning to use his hand, to nod a little with his head, would be an effort on his part and of those around him that was greater than scaling the highest peak.
Maybe he'd never travel to see that sunset, but a light shone from his eyes that would dazzle any star. He couldn't sail or steer a rudder, but he could lead others to calm waters in the stormiest seas.

I was immersed in all of these new sensations, when I suddenly felt a movement, a small tug. It was the cord! It was only hanging by a thread. Where was my sweet jailer?

No! I couldn't go now, I had so many things to do together with Yago. Not now!
"Let's go and have a swim, Yago. Nap time's over."

There was no way out. If I didn't fall off from the cord wearing out, the first wave would tear me off, and I'd be cast back into the sea. Maybe I'd find another friend one day, but Yago...

And if I made it in time? I wanted to be hopeful, when really there was no hope left. We were walking into the water on dad's shoulders, and there was a great commotion. Yago got into the water, as his whole body shivered and trembled with excitement.

And then...I felt a tug on the cord, this time the last. Farewell, Yago, farewell to my silent friend who spoke from the depths of his heartbeats. Farewell to the child with the eyes that reflected the most beautiful emotions, farewell to my dearest, most sincere companion, and...

What was this? A new heartbeat! Different, as deep as the sea, gentle as the waves on the shore, as playful as the tide as it ebbs and flows... it was me! It was my heartbeat! Yago had a heartbeat for me!

He greeted me, he said goodbye to me; in his heartbeat I understood how much he had been grateful for my company, how much...

Yago!

I slid off without a sound, without being able to warn anyone.

The cord snapped, and I returned to the sea.

"Over there, over there! Can you see it? Run and get it before it sinks!"

"I've got it mum, I've got it!"

"Good boy, Guille. We nearly lost her. Look, I've brought this wonderful strong leather cord with a clasp, so he'll never lose it again."

Never. Hanging forever around the neck of the silent child. Silent?

I'm happy to be a sea snail hanging around the neck of a little boy. I'm lucky to be able to share his inner cries and silence. I feel proud to share my life with another who seems to be missing so much, but in the end has everything.

I hope to spend many years together with Yago, smelling the fresh scent of the flowers that Marta brings to him, laughing at Guille's adventures, growing with the strength and unconditional love of his father, and letting myself drift away with the melodies and endless caresses of his mother.

But above all, listening to the orchestra of heartbeats that rises from deep within his heart.